NIHILISM REVISED

PRESENTS

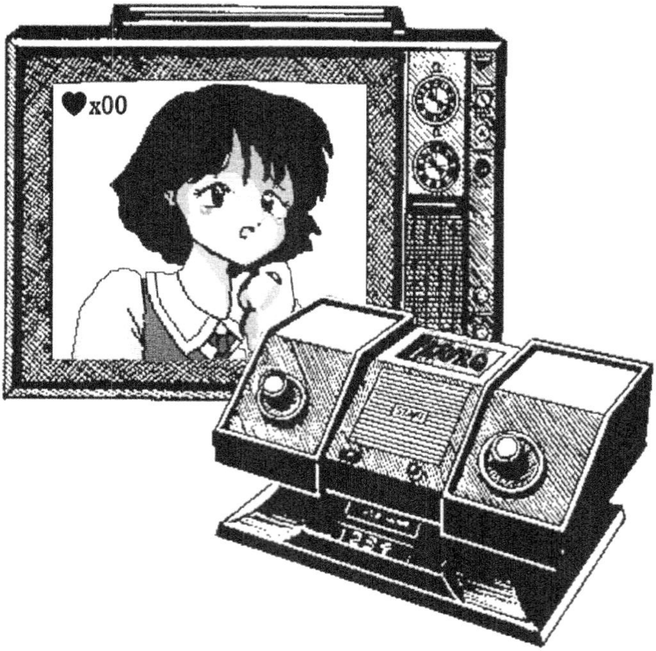
x00

BEN ARZATE

THE COMPLETE IDIOT'S GUIDE
TO SAYING GOODBYE

▶ START
OPTIONS

Dedicated to Darrell and Marge Jurmu

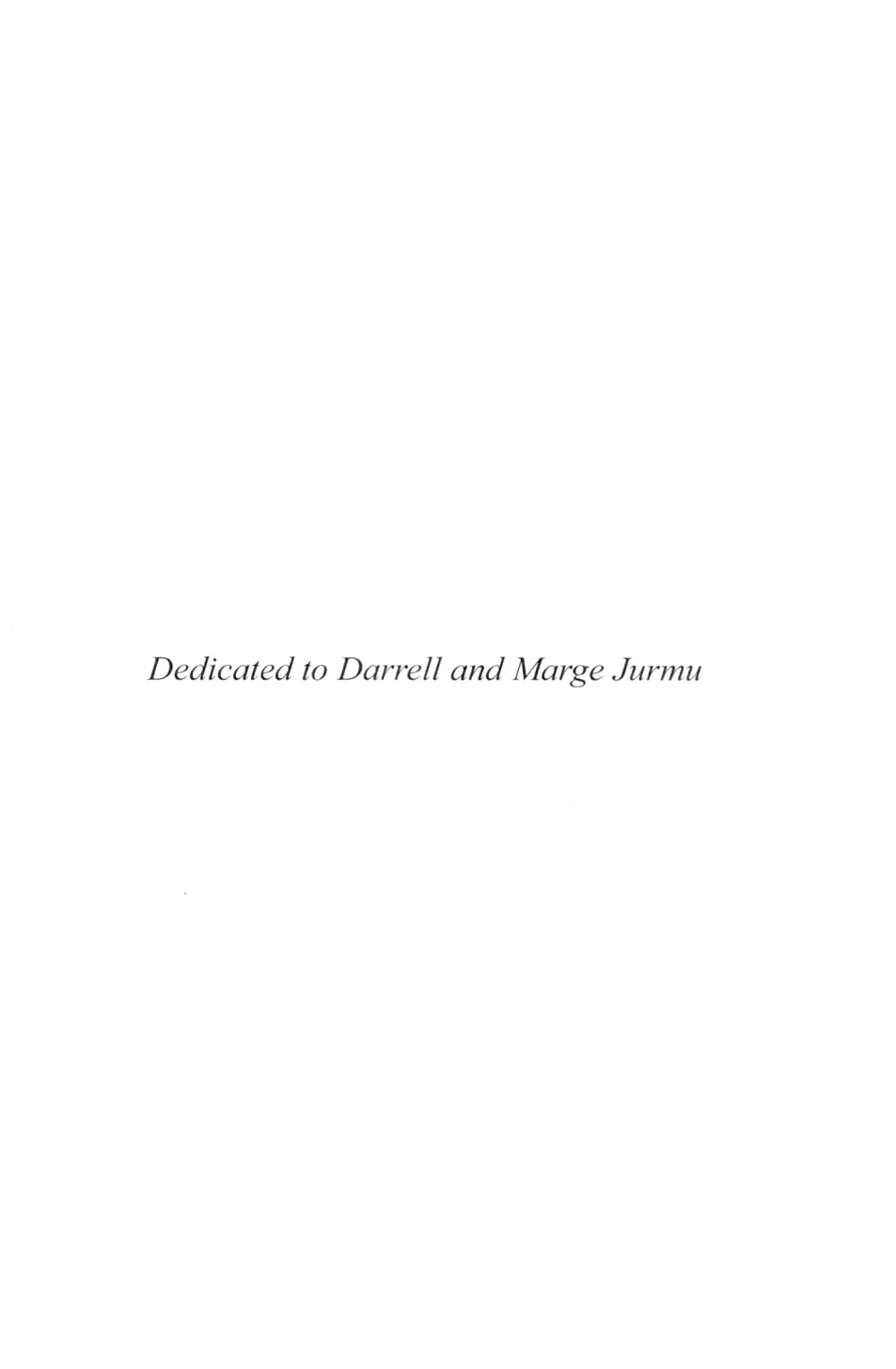

"'Truth,' said a traveller,
'Is a breath, a wind,
'A shadow, a phantom;
'Long have I pursued it,
'But never have I touched
'The hem of its garment.'"

— Stephen Crane, *Black Riders and Other Lines*

"Is there anything of which one can say,
'Look! This is something new'?
It was here already, long ago;
it was here before our time.
No one remembers the former generations,
and even those yet to come
will not be remembered
by those who follow them."

— Ecclesiastes 1:10-11

"The passion for destruction is a creative passion, too!"

— Mikhail Bakunin, *The Reaction in Germany*

STORY SELECTION

This Be the Creation Story **1**

The Country Musician **3**

The Arranged Marriage **7**

Alex Buys Coffee **19**

… but i was reminded of … **20**

The Rent is Due **23**

The Obese Man Goes on a Diet.......................... **24**

The Soda **25**

The Complete Idiot's Guide to Saying
Goodbye **29**

Meth Lab Nursery.. **31**

Channel 104 at 2:45 AM **39**

Two Sentence Horror Story.................................**40**

Alex Checks the Mail...**41**

Violent Bitch Hitomi..**42**

My Church **52**

WATER MUSIC...**54**

Unreflected Text...**55**

The Akihabara Strangler **58**

Please File Under Adult Contemporary **60**

Sharp-Tongued **64**

There Goes the Neighborhood **65**

RealDoll Ballet...**70**

John Walks into a Bar	**72**
Cathy	**78**
Little Jimmy's Secret	**80**
Why You Should Always Tip the Pizza Guy	**83**
Last Night I Dreamt of Hell and High Waters	**84**
Deep Sea Diving Suit	**88**
Human Roach	**90**
Alex Watches Television	**91**
A Very Young Something with Wings	**94**
War Criminal: A One Act Play for One Performer	**96**
Love: A Parable	**99**

This Be the Creation Story

In the beginning God was sitting on His couch in His underwear. Why a divine being would need to sit and why He would bother with underwear when He was the only being that existed are questions to be left to the theologians.

God was feeling depressed because He was lonely. He was thinking about creating some other beings who He could be friends with and who could invent the television so He could watch it. He could have created the TV Himself, but with no actors, writers, and producers, there wouldn't be anything on it.

The problem was God had really low self-esteem and figured if He created anything, He would just fuck it all up. He thought that if He created people, they wouldn't want to be His friends and would make really shitty TV shows. He thought about for a bit and decided there was no point in continuing to exist.

So, God created a gun and put it to the side of His head. He shut his eyes and pulled the trigger.

And so, God died, but His blood, brain meat, and fragments of His skull remained to fly out into the void. Then gravity and all the shit that made the universe what it is today took effect and everything you know, including yourself, is here now. Consult a science textbook if you want all the specific details.

Looking around now, it seems like God was right to have no confidence in His creation abilities.

The Country Musician

He calls himself Hank. His last name is not Williams. He wishes it were. His birth name is not Henry. His birth name is Jordan. He has always hated the name Jordan. He prefers to be called Hank. We will respect his wishes and call him Hank.

Hank is a struggling country musician. He recorded five songs in his home and burned them on a CD. He sent the CD to a record company. The record company gave him a deal and had him sign a contract. A week later the company was bought out. The new owners ignored his contract and calls. The new owners changed the company so that its only output was novelty techno songs. The songs were all made by the same anonymous studio musicians working under different band names. The songs were pulled from stores and the radio when they were all found to induce vomiting and seizures. The company shut down soon afterwards.

Hank put the five songs on the Internet. After a year, each has less than 300 plays. None of them have gotten any plays in the past month. Hank burned two more CDs and sent them to two different record companies. Both sent back letters saying Hank should come visit them in person.

Hank is visiting both record companies today. He puts on his cowboy hat, grabs his guitar, and walks to the first company.

The receptionist has him go in the office right away. He walks in and shakes hands with the record executive. The executive is young and wears a green suit.

The executive tells Hank that he liked his demo, but country is out. He says that reggae is the next big thing.

Hank tells the executive that he likes reggae, but he does not play reggae. He plays country. He also says he is not black and not Jamaican.

The executive tells him that it does not matter that he is not black. There are white Jamaicans. In a voice that sounds like Santa Claus, he says that Hank just has to do a fake Jamaican accent. He puts his hands on his belly and says "ho ho ho" after every sentence. The executive says that it is so easy, he is doing it right now. He tells Hank that they will just say he is a white Jamaican. Nobody looks into these things. He tells Hank to give it a try.

Hank looks at the executive. He blinks twice, then turns around and leaves.

Hank goes to the next record company. The receptionist has him wait in the lobby for an hour, then she tells him to go in the office. The record executive is old, wears a black suit, and holds a cow femur in his left hand. He has a very angry look on his face. Hank is afraid to approach him for a handshake.

The record executive taps on his desk with the cow femur. Hank recognizes it as Morse code.

The executive is asking if he wants a record deal with them.

Hank says yes.

The executive sits doing nothing, then taps the same question but louder.

Hanks taps yes on his guitar.

The executive taps that he wants Hank to play a song.

Hank plays one of his songs.

When he is done, the executive taps to ask if Hank is going to play a song or not.

Hank plays the song again, but instead of singing, he taps the lyrics with his foot.

The executive taps that they do not sign a cappella acts.

Hank thinks about playing the song again, tapping the chords with his left foot and the lyrics with his right foot. Instead, he turns around and leaves.

Hank decides to busk in the park for the rest of the day. He finds a spot, puts his cowboy hat on the ground, and begins playing. After half an hour, several people have walked by, but no one has put any money in the hat.

A cop approaches Hank. He asks Hank if he has a permit.

Hank says he does not. He asks if he will get a ticket.

The cop says that the city has introduced a new penalty for busking without a permit.

Hank walks home with the neck of his guitar shoved up his ass. He gets home and pulls it out. He sits on his couch. It hurts to sit, so he stands up.

Hank begins to feel discouraged. He decides to cheer himself up by playing an acoustic country arrangement of Jimmy Cliff's "You Can Get It If You Really Want." He stops when he realizes he is singing in a fake Jamaican accent.

The Arranged Marriage

"Congratulations on your marriage!" my mom said to me as I walked in the door. She was standing in the kitchen with my dad, the girl from across the street, and her parents.

"What?" I said.

My dad pushed the girl towards me. She had a blank expression. "Meet Mrs. Michael C!" he said.

I looked at the girl. She was a head shorter than me and had curly brown hair. I looked at my parents. "What's going on?" I said.

The girl's father frowned. "He's not taking this as well as you said he would," he said to my parents.

"Oh, don't worry. He's just surprised," my dad said.

"Yes. Very," I said. "What is going on?"

"Oh, honey," my mom said, "Lisa was already set up with someone. Unfortunately, he can't marry her anymore. Her parents told us all about at it and we knew you would make a great husband for her, so we went ahead and filed all the paperwork!"

Oh, Lisa. That was the girl's name.

"Isn't she like 16? I mean, I'm only 18," I said.

"That's no problem," Lisa's mom said. "That's when I married her father."

"I don't even know her," I said.

"Don't worry," Lisa's mom said. "You can get to know her over your honeymoon."

"Honeymoon?" I said. "I'm trying to save for college. I don't want to spend the money to travel somewhere."

"You don't need to. Just take her out to the carnival tomorrow," Lisa's dad said.

"Isn't that more like a date than a honeymoon?" I said.

"You worry too much, Michael," my mom said. "You'll be a great husband. Just be loyal and caring and everything will be fine. Now, let's go to your bride's house to have dinner and celebrate!"

Lisa's parents led the way across the street, followed by my parents and Lisa and I behind them all. I looked over at Lisa, but she kept facing forward with that same blank expression.

We got to Lisa's home and her mother made dinner. She served roast beef, mashed potatoes, green beans with cheese, and biscuits. Our parents kept talking about how happy they were for us, but Lisa and I didn't say a word. Her parents had us do the dishes afterward. Again, we said nothing to each other.

After we finished the dishes we went into the living room where our parents were sitting. After a few awkward minutes of sitting next to each other, Lisa's dad spoke up.

"Well, I think you two should be off to bed," he said.

"It's only eight," I said.

"It's your wedding night. You and your wife should go to bed now."

With that, he led us into a bedroom with a large bed and not much else.

"Good night!" he said and closed the door on us.

I looked at Lisa. "Is this your room?" I said.

"No, it's a guest bedroom," she said.

"Why are they having us sleep here?"

"I don't think they had us sleeping in mind."

"Huh?"

"It's our wedding night. They want us to have sex."

"Oh."

I stared at her for a moment.

"Aren't you going to get undressed?" I said.

"Aren't you?"

"Okay."

I started to undress. Lisa just sat on the bed. I motioned at her and said, "Uh."

"Help me undress," she said.

I stripped down to my boxers and went over to her. I kissed her, but she didn't kiss back. She went along with me taking her clothes off though. When she was naked, she got on her back and spread her legs. I took my boxers off. I was only half hard and had to jerk myself into a full hard-on. I entered her and she moaned and closed her eyes. After about five minutes of fucking her, I started losing my boner. I shut my eyes and thought about my English teacher. I finally came inside her after that. I rolled off of her. She sighed and stared up at the ceiling.

"Hey," I said. "Was that your first time?"

"No, but don't tell my parents that," she said.

"I won't."

I rolled over and stared at the wall until I fell asleep

I woke up with morning wood. I thought about waking up Lisa and having sex with her again. I decided against it and just got in the shower and jerked off. When I came out, Lisa had woken up and was waiting to use the bathroom. We exchanged glances and she went in without saying anything. I got dressed and went in the dining room. Lisa's mother had made a breakfast of sausage, eggs, hash browns, coffee, and orange juice.

"Is Lisa awake?" Lisa's mother said.

"Yeah. She's taking a shower," I said.

Lisa walked in and joined us at the table. Lisa's father and my parents came in right after. While we ate, they talked about how well they thought we would hit it off at our honeymoon/first date.

"Are you looking forward to going to the carnival?" I asked Lisa.

"I guess," she said.

"Yeah," I said.

We finished our breakfast and headed out. Our parents waved to us from the porch as we walked to the carnival. I looked over at Lisa. She was staring straight ahead as she walked next to me.

"Hey," I said to her, "what happened to the guy you were engaged to before?"

"He had this weird disease," she said.

"Oh, I'm sorry. Did he die?"

"Not yet. But he will soon."

"I'm sorry to hear that. Are you sad?"

"Yeah."

"Did you love him?"

"I guess."

"How long were you engaged to him?"

"Since I was ten."

"Wow."

"Yeah. He was a pretty great guy."

"Are you sad you had to marry me?"

"Kind of. Sorry if that sounds mean."

"No, no. I understand. I'll do what I can to make this painless."

"Thanks."

We got to the carnival grounds and I bought our tickets. We walked past the tents and stands. We stopped in front of a shooting gallery. The man standing in the booth was wearing a lab coat with fake blood and he had white makeup all over his face. The targets ran along on a conveyor belt behind him. They were painted on glass vials with different colored liquids in them. The sign above it read "Mad Science Mutation."

"Good morning, young man!" the carny said. "Why don't you try your hand and win a prize for your lovely girlfriend?"

"She's my wife, actually." I said.

The carny looked at Lisa, then back at me. He raised one of his eyebrows. "Well then!" he said and cleared his throat. "Want to try your luck and win a prize for your lovely wife?"

I looked around the booth. "I don't see any prizes."

The carny reached under the counter and pulled out a cage. There was an animal inside that looked kind of like a shaved rat.

"What I'll do is release this little feller in that little track under the targets. The goal is to hit the vials and spill the mutation chemicals on him. It's five dollars a shot. If you hit him and mutate him, you get to keep him!" the carny said.

"That won't hurt it, will it?" I said.

"Not at all, I assure you!"

I didn't really believe him, but I gave him ten dollars. He took the rat thing out of the cage and set it down under the targets. It ran back and forth, trapped by the bars on either side. I took the air rifle from the carny. On the first shot, I missed the targets completely. On the second shot, I got lucky. Not only did I hit the target, but the rat thing was right under it. The white liquid spilled out and covered it. It rolled into a ball and made a squeaking sound. It sounded like it was in pain and I felt really bad. I looked over at Lisa and she was just staring at it.

The rat thing started growing white fur all over its body. After a few minutes, it stopped twitching and squeaking. The carny picked it up and brought it over to us. It seemed to be fine now. It went from looking a shaved rat to a combination of a fluffy baby rabbit and a mouse. It actually looked really cute.

"It eats any kind of vegetable," the carny said. "Feed it at least twice a day. Congratulations!"

I held the bunny mouse for a minute and handed it over to Lisa. She hugged it to her chest. "It's really cute, thank you."

When she said that she actually smiled. That was the first time I'd seen her do that. Something about it felt forced.

We walked away from the booth. We went to a stage towards the center of the carnival. On the stage, there was a robot playing guitar and a guy dressed up as flamboyant cowboy. They were performing George Jones's "White Lightning."

"I love this song," I said to Lisa. "I suppose you don't like country music?"

"I hate it," she said.

"What kind of music do you listen to?"

"Nothing specific. I usually just turn on the radio and browse around until I find something I like."

"What do you usually like?"

"It depends on what mood I'm in."

She hugged the bunny mouse to her chest again. She stood there with me and we listened to the band play a couple more songs. We walked around some more and passed by the concession stands. "You want something to eat?" I said.

"No, I'm still full from breakfast."

"Yeah, I am too."

We passed by a gyro stand and I asked them for some lettuce. I gave it to Lisa and she fed it to the bunny mouse. It was pretty adorable watching it nibble on the lettuce.

"Are you going to name him?" I said.

"Why would I do that?"

We walked past a tent with a sign in front that read "FREAK SHOW" in big letters. Underneath it said, "Inside You'll See: Hans the Nazi Horse! Mr. Comic Character! Brad the Oldest 17 Year Old In The World! Fast Forward Boy! The Stringless Guitar Player! And More!"

When Lisa read the sign, she grabbed me and hurried me into the tent.

"Hey, what's the matter? Did you want to see this that bad?" I said.

She didn't say anything. I glanced at the freaks on display in their stalls. There was a guy who moved around like someone on a tape being fast forwarded, a horse with swastikas all over its body, a guy with small mouths where his eyes should be, a guy who mimed strumming on a stringless guitar and sang what sounded like guitar notes, a man in a suit with blank flesh where his face should be, and a woman with a gash in her throat that looked like a vagina. Lisa finally stopped dragging me along in front of one of the exhibits.

It was an old man sitting on a stool. I looked at the sign in front of the big stall he was in. It read, "Meet Brad! He looks 80, but he's really 17! Don't believe us? Ask him and he'll give you proof!"

"Brad! Brad it's me!" Lisa said.

The old man raised his head and looked at her. He stood up with wide eyes and hobbled over to her. She sat the bunny mouse on the ground and they hugged each other.

"Do you two know each other?" I said.

"Michael, this is my ex-fiancé."

"I thought you said he got a disease."

"I do have a disease," Brad said. "This is what it did to me."

"Made you age really fast? I've never heard of that."

"It's really rare," Lisa said.

"Huh. Why are you here?" I said.

"I took this job to save some money for Lisa before I died. Who are you?" Brad said.

"My parents made me marry him," Lisa said.

"They did? Those idiots. I told them not to do this."

"I'm sorry about what happened to you," I said. "I'll try to take care of her."

"Do you even want to be married to her?" Brad said.

"Not really," I said. "No offense, Lisa."

"It's okay," Lisa said. "I didn't want to marry you either."

"Why didn't you just get an annulment?" Brad said.

"I didn't know I could that," I said.

"You're not very smart, are you?"

"Hey, screw you."

"Calm down. Look, I'll just tell the boss I'm taking my break. I'll take you both to the courthouse and show you how to do it."

"My parents aren't going to be happy," Lisa said.

"Yeah, mine neither," I said

"You'll both have to deal with that if you don't want to stay in this marriage." Brad said.

"I guess so," Lisa said.

"Come on," Brad said. He walked towards the exit of the tent. Lisa took his hand and followed him by his side.

I saw the bunny mouse scurrying around in circles on the ground. I picked it up and followed the two out of the tent.

Alex Buys Coffee

Alex holds the coin up. He looks at the face on it. He turns the coin. He looks at the face from different angles. He grasps the coin in his palm. He walks over to the coffee machine. He puts the coin in the machine. He selects the option for black coffee. A coffee cup drops from the machine. It fills up. Alex takes the cup of coffee. He drinks the coffee. He feels it drop into the inside of his feet. He keeps drinking until he feels himself filled to the top of his skull. He crumples the cup. He throws it in a nearby garbage bin.

Alex walks over to a bench. He sits down. He takes a ten-dollar bill out of his pocket. He folds it into an origami butterfly. The origami butterfly begins to flutter its wings. It flies off. Alex tries to grab it. It moves too fast. The origami butterfly flies out of the park and into the city. It flies into the slums. It lands on a bum sleeping on the sidewalk. The bum wakes up. He grabs the origami butterfly and unfolds it. He goes into a nearby liquor store. He buys a bottle of whiskey. He goes back to his spot on the sidewalk. He drinks from the bottle.

... but I was reminded of ...

I sit in the diner.

I take a bite of my food.

At the next booth, a man is sitting on the table.

He has no shoes, he's dirty all over, and his hair looks like asbestos.

He rocks back and forth with a coffee mug in his hand.

The servers won't go near him.

He brought the mug in with him.

I don't think there's anything in it.

But he keeps taking sips.

My server comes up and pours me another cup of coffee.

Her cheeks are attached to her ears with hooks.

It creates an awful permanent smile.

The tables in the diner are mirrors.

I look away when I eat.

I don't like watching myself eat.

Outside, the sky is mostly clear with a few clouds.

There is a loud noise.

The sky shatters.

Blue and white fragments of firmament fall to the ground like glass shards.

Now it's dark.

I can see my reflection in the diner's windows.

I don't like so many reflections of myself.

I look around the diner.

It's pretty crowded.

But I still feel lonely.

At one table, an emaciated woman with several empty plates around her is ordering more food.

Across from her sits a morbidly obese woman eating a tiny salad.

The cook sticks his head out of the kitchen door to talk to one of the servers about something.

His skin is burned so badly that it resembles hamburger meat.

I want to leave.

I quickly finish the last of my food.

My server comes over with the check.

It's printed on the back of a photograph.

I turn it over.

The photograph is of the server naked with her legs spread.

My bill is $8.50.

I leave a $10.

The last of my money.

Outside, the pieces of glass crunch beneath my shoes like snow.

I look up.

The stars hanging in the night are arranged in a grid.

They can't form any constellations except basic shapes.

I look left and right.

The road goes for miles in both directions.

There are no other buildings except the diner.

I'm in a desert.

I don't remember how I got here.

I don't have a car.

I reach up and pluck the moon out its place.

I flip it like a coin.

Light side, I walk left.

Dark side, I walk right.

The Rent is Due

On the first of every month, every tenant in our building is awoken at 3:30 AM. This is the signal to come down to the foyer to pay our rent.

Once we are down in the foyer, the landlord takes a head count. If someone is missing, the landlord will seek them out. He refuses to begin until everyone is present.

When all the tenants are there, he will then strap a thick book to his face with a belt. It's usually the state tax code, but sometimes it will be a dictionary. At least once, it was a hardcover copy of *The Brothers Karamazov*.

The landlord will then walk among us. Each of must hit the book with our fist at least once. If he's unsatisfied with the punch one of us gave, he will tap them on the shoulder to let them know to give him another one.

When everyone has beaten the book to his satisfaction, he will remove it to reveal his bruised and swollen face. He thanks us all and leaves, telling us he will see us all next month.

Some choose to go back to bed after this. I prefer to get a head start on my day.

The Obese Man Goes on a Diet

The obese man decides to lose weight. He decides he will only eat foods that are not fattening from now on.

He goes into the kitchen to have dinner, but finds he only has donuts. He cuts the holes out of the donuts and has a meal of them. He finds them tasty, though unfilling.

The next morning, the obese man wakes up to a sharp pain in his abdomen. He clutches his gut and writhes on the bed. The pain is so bad that he reaches for a phone and calls an ambulance.

The ambulance takes the obese man to the hospital, but he dies before he arrives.
During the autopsy, the coroner determines that the cause of death was several holes in the walls of the obese man's stomach and intestines.

The Soda

Five years ago, a mysterious brand of soda began appearing in supermarkets and convenience stores all over the world. It seems to appear on the shelves of the stores out of thin air. All store owners and employees that have been asked have no recollection of ordering or stocking the soda. It always comes in glass bottles with no labels on them and a white cap. There has never been an individual one spotted on a shelf, only six packs. The packaging is also blank white save for the word "soda" in black bold letters on the front and back. There is no other identifying information save for the bar code or the store's price tag. Attempts to trace the bar codes have so far turned up nothing. The price has always been the same on all sightings of the mysterious soda, the equivalent of $4 USD. It always shows up on receipts and check-out machines as simply "soda."

The most peculiar thing is that each individual bottle seems to have its own unusual properties. The soda itself always resembles a simple cola, but rarely does it actually taste like it. Or even act like it. For example, in one particular six pack:

- Bottle 1 was described as tasting like water.
- Bottle 2 tasted like hot coffee despite no heat coming from the bottle or the soda itself.
- Bottle 3's soda turned into worms after it was opened.
- Bottle 4 tasted like cola, but the bottle was found to be able to see though walls when looked through like a telescope.
- Bottle 5 shattered and the soda inside disappeared when it was opened.
- Bottle 6's soda turned solid when it was opened. After breaking open the bottle, it was found to have become candle wax.

This six pack was observed in early 2008 when the soda first started appearing. During this time, it was believed that as unusual as this phenomenon was, it could be written off as benign. However, as time goes on, the soda seems to become increasingly dangerous.

The first reported incident of someone harmed by it was in March of 2010. An elderly man in Madrid arrived at a local hospital complaining of severe abdominal pain. While waiting for care, the man vomited up fecal matter. Testing showed that his bowels were severely obstructed. Immediate surgery was required. After further questioning, it was found the man's condition could be directly attributed to drinking a bottle of the mysterious soda.

The first reported incident of death caused by the soda was in January of 2011. A family of five in Osaka were found dead in their home of mustard gas poisoning. The gas had been released from a bottle of the soda. Two months later, a Chicago convenience store clerk working the night shift was found dead behind the counter with eight rounds of .22 caliber bullets in his head. Security footage showed that the bullets had shot out of a bottle of the soda the clerk had opened. It was concluded these were no longer isolated incidents when, three months later, a young woman in Buenos Aires had her face melted off by acid sprayed at her by one of the bottles.

Word was put out as far and wide as possible to never open the bottles and for them to be turned over to authorities should they be spotted. Earlier this year, the full extent of the soda's danger was observed in a small town in Ecuador. From what could be gathered from survivors, an owner of a local market had found a six pack of the soda and (against the advice of onlookers) was disposing of it by putting the bottles in a garbage bag and smashing it on the street. The bottles breaking resulted in an explosion that destroyed most of the town. The area is now uninhabitable due to fall out, the bottles apparently having had the same effect as a nuclear bomb.

Governments all over the world are taking action to seize and safely store as many bottles as possible. However, due to the nature of the soda's appearance, there is no way to trace them all and no way to keep them out of private hands even with the strictest of penalties for possession.

To make matters worse, the bottles seem to be appearing more and more often. Last week, in supermarkets in Quebec, Mexico City, Seoul, and Johannesburg, the staff came in to find all of their inventory had disappeared and been replaced by six packs of the mysterious soda.

The Complete Idiot's Guide to Saying Goodbye

The news hit us pretty hard. We knew what it probably was, but we hoped we were wrong. We knew for certain now. Our house had cancer.

It started when my son fell down the stairs. Thankfully, he was fine besides a few bruises. He said he tripped over a lump in the carpet. I went up the stairs and saw the lump. There were several more on the railing. I told my wife that this could be serious and we called an inspector.

The inspector came over while my wife and I were at work and our son at school. When we all got back, the inspector was waiting for us out front. He gave us the bad news.

He said it looked like the tumors had probably started up in the attic. Had we found it then, it might have been treatable. But it had spread too much at that point.

I still can't help but blame myself. A house that old was very prone to disease. I should have had him checked on a regular basis.

The only thing we could do now was have him put down.

We found a two-bedroom apartment near downtown. It was much smaller, but it would fit our needs. We moved as fast as we could. We didn't want our old house to suffer too long.

I scheduled the demolition. It would be a quick and painless implosion. On the day the crew came to do it, we went over to say goodbye.

Our son was probably hit the hardest. After all, he lived there since he was born. We sat in the empty living room. My wife and I reminisced on when we first moved in after we got married.

The crew told us that everything was rigged and it was time to leave. We got in the car. My son was bawling. My wife had tears running down her cheeks. I kept having to wipe my eyes as I started the car.

As we drove off, we heard the loud rumbling. Then the sound of debris falling. Then nothing.

<u>Meth Lab Nursery</u>

Scott opens the door to his apartment and goes inside. He immediately hears his son crying loudly. He looks over and sees his wife is asleep on the couch. He goes to her and begins to shake her.

"Hey! Hey, can't you hear that hear that?" he says.

His wife stirs. When she opens her eyes, the white heavily contrasts with the dark circles around them. She moans and closes her eyes again.

"Hey! Wake up, Mary!" he says as he shakes her harder.

"What?" Mary says. She doesn't open her eyes. She scratches her head. Her hair is thinning.

"Can you not hear that?" He points down the hall at his son's room.

"You take care of him. I don't feel good." She rubs her face.

"Goddammit."

Scott walks down the hall. The door to his son's room is open. He kicks an empty drain cleaner bottle on the floor in front of him. It goes under his son's crib. It makes a loud noise as it hits the wall. His son starts crying louder.

"Goddammit," he says.

He leans in to pick him up. A strong smell makes he pull back. He clenches his teeth and begins breathing through his mouth. He leans down and picks up his son. He sees there is a brown stain where his son was laying. He sighs and lays his son back down.

He goes back down the hall and into the kitchen. He opens a cupboard under the counter and grabs a diaper, wipes, and baby powder. He goes back in his son's room. He cleans his son and puts on the new diaper. He takes the diaper and throws it in the garbage can next to the makeshift lab in the room. He is amazed at how much shit was in it and wonders when Mary last changed him.

He takes his son out of the crib and sets him on the floor. His son is still crying. He picks up the crib mattress and flips it over. He picks his son up and rocks him in his arms.

"Come on, stop crying. Stop crying," he says.

He takes his son into the living room. His wife is still asleep on the couch. He turns on the TV. He puts in a DVD of *Teletubbies* and sits on the chair next to the couch. He bounces his son on his knee until he stops crying

Scott sits in his truck. He is at the outskirts of town. He looks at his watch. It reads 1:36 AM. He is startled by someone knocking on his window. He sees that it is the man he was waiting for. He rolls down his window.

"You got the shit?" the man says.

The man is jittery. His face is sunken. He wears a ratty baseball cap.

"Keep it down, stupid ass," Scott says.

"Just give me it, man."

"Give me the money first."

The man reaches in his pocket and pulls out a wad of bills. He hands it to Scott. Scott counts it and when he finds there is enough, he stuffs it in his pocket. He reaches over and opens the glove box. He pulls out a small sandwich bag with crystals in it. He hands it to the man.

"Hey, this is way less than usual," the man says.

"So? They're cracking down. It's harder to get the shit I need," Scott says.

"Then give me some money back, man"

"How 'bout you fuck off and I won't smash in your goddamn mouth?"

The man holds up his middle finger and walks away. Scott starts up his truck. The song "Bless the Broken Road" by Rascal Flatts plays on the radio as he drives home.

He parks his truck and goes inside. Mary is sitting on the couch. She smiles at him. She is missing several teeth. "Everything go all right, honey?" she says.

"Yeah, all good," Scott says.

"You ready for bed, dear?"

"Yeah"

She gets up and leads him down the hall to the bedroom. Scott looks at the door to his son's room.

"Is Mark asleep?" Scott says.

"Yeah, he's been asleep awhile," Mary says.

"You changed him and everything, didn't you?"

"Yes, stop worrying."

Scott looks at the door to Mark's room again. He and Mary go inside their bedroom. They undress. Mary is very thin. There are spots all over her body. She kisses Scott. It tastes really foul to him. He lays on the bed and she climbs on top of him. She rides him until he cums inside of her. She climbs off him. While Scott lays next to Mary he can feel her toss and turn. He falls asleep.

He wakes up to Mary climbing on top of him. He goes in and out of sleep while she rides on him. When he finally cums, he is fully awakened. He keeps his eyes closed and eventually falls back asleep. He is again awoken by the sound of Mark crying. He sits up and yawns. Mary, who is already up, tells him to go back to sleep and that she will take care of Mark. He lays back down. For a brief moment, he feels worried. He dismisses his worries and goes back to sleep.

Scott wakes up. Mary is not next to him. He hears Mark crying. He walks over to Mark's room and briefly wonders where Mary is. He thinks to himself that she disappears all the time. He picks up Mark, takes him into the kitchen, and puts him in a high chair. He feeds Mark before making himself toast. When he finishes eating, he gives Mark some toys. He opens a cupboard under the sink and grabs a dust mask and some rubber gloves. He goes back into Mark's room. He goes over to the makeshift lab and goes to work. After about a half hour, the doorbell rings.

"Goddammit," he says.

He throws off his mask and gloves. He closes the door to Mark's room and goes to the front door. It is the apartment manager with his teenage grandson.

"I've been getting complaints about weird smells coming from here," the manager says.

"No one's said anything to me," Scott says.

"I'm saying something to you now. What's going on?"

"Nothing. I'm just taking care of my kid."

"Why aren't you at work?"

"My wife works."

"Have you noticed any weird smells?"

"No."

"Why are you the only one? Both your neighbors have complained."

"I don't know."

"Are you trying to hide something?"

"What would I hide?"

"Something that might get your ass kicked out."

"Don't threaten me."

"Then stop being difficult."

"I'm not."

"You are. You're not doing yourself any favors."

The manager's grandson taps him on the shoulder. "We'd better hurry, Grandpa. We told Jeff we'd be there by five."

"If I get another complaint. I'm coming in to inspect the apartment. Consider this your notice," the manager says. He and his grandson walk back to their truck.

Scott closes the door and hold up his middle finger at it. He goes back to Mark's room. He decides he will worry about the apartment manager later. He picks up the dust mask and gloves and goes back to work.

Scott sits on the couch watching TV. Mary comes in the living room.

"I need to take the truck," she says.

"What for?" he says

"I got an appointment on the other side of town," she says.

Scott pauses for a moment. "Okay. Put some gas in the truck while you're out."

He gives her the keys and some money.

"I'll be back in the morning," she says. "Mark's asleep, so don't worry about him."

She leaves. Scott wonders who she's going to fuck. He wonders if he is better looking than him. He decides that he wouldn't need to hire Mary if that was the case. He wonders if he is uglier than him. He wonders if he is older than him. He imagines an ugly, old man thrusting on top of her while she cringes underneath him. He feels his cock get hard. He takes off his clothes and lays on the couch. He jacks off until he cums on his belly and chest. He falls asleep.

Scott wakes up to the sound of Mark's crying. He gets up. While he puts on his pants he smells smoke. He runs back to Mark's room. He throws open the door and is hit with thick smoke. He cannot see into the room. The heat is intense. He coughs and stumbles away. He grabs his cell phone and runs outside. He dials 911. He says there is a fire and gives his address.

He thinks about running back inside to get Mark. But he knows he won't make it. He thinks about getting in the truck and running away. But he remembers that Mary has the truck. He sits on the curb in nothing but his pants. People are running outside. He covers his face with his hands. There is yelling. Scott can hear the fire truck sirens.

Channel 104 at 2:45 AM

The broadcast opens on an almost empty television studio. The only thing in the studio is a man in a lawn chair.

He looks to be around forty years old. He wears blue jeans and a gray button-up shirt. His feet are bare.

He watches a TV.

Sometimes he laughs. Sometimes he cries. Sometimes he curses at the screen.

The viewer cannot see what is on his TV.

The broadcast lasts about fifteen minutes.

Two Sentence Horror Story

It's not that she keeps texting me that bothers me. It's that when I go to visit her, she's still in the coma.

Alex Checks the Mail

Alex enters his apartment building. He goes to a wall of cuckoo clocks. He goes to the clock that is at 2:11. He turns the clock hands to noon. A keyhole appears in the center of the clock. Alex takes out his keys. He puts a key in the hole. A bird comes out of the clock. It makes a cuckoo noise. The clock chimes. The bird has Alex's mail in its beak. Alex takes his mail. The bird goes back in the clock. The clock hands go back to 2:11. Alex goes upstairs to his apartment.

Violent Bitch Hitomi

Hitomi put her thick glasses on and went out to the balcony. She picked up the Harlequin romance novel on the chair, sat down, and started reading. Across the street, a building was being reconstructed. She often wondered how that office building got leveled in the Great Collapse but this dingy apartment building was somehow almost untouched. The roof got fucked up and it was without power for a year, but that was nothing compared to what happened through most of the city.

Hitomi sat reading. She got lost in the fantasy on the pages until she was snapped out by the barking and yelling that came from up the street. She peered over the balcony. Jack came into view and ran across the parking lot below her. The black hound crouched down and sprang up. It hopped the two floors and landed on the balcony. Hitomi kneeled, looking down at the black dog's three eyes and scratching his head to calm him.

"What's going on, Jack?" she said.

Jack responded. She had never gotten used to the way he spoke. Most heard it as just barking. Hitomi heard it both as barking and speaking. It was like she was wearing a pair of headphones where nothing but barks came through the left ear while clear English came in through the right.

"You've got to get downtown, Hitomi!" Jack said, accompanied by barks. "Some G.E.T members got a hold of a Neohuman and took over the Radford Credit Union building! They're turning the place into a damn slaughterhouse!"

The God of the End Times cult. They were a bunch of psychos who believed that the Great Collapse was the first stage of the return of God and they were the chosen people to bring about the end of humanity and begin the Final Judgment. They were probably the most dangerous of all the groups that popped up after the Collapse. They were set on human genocide and had no fear of death whatsoever. They were fanatics convinced they'd be sent straight to heaven.

Hitomi nodded. She ran back inside and threw the book on the bed. She sat the glasses on her dresser and pulled her jeans and T-shirt off, revealing a bright red leotard with several rips under her clothes. She ran back out on the balcony as Jack jumped off. She grabbed the railing of the balcony and flipped over it, landing next to Jack on her feet.

Jack took off past the parking lot and down the road with Hitomi following close behind. As

Jack began to outrun her, Hitomi dropped to all fours and began catching up. The black and red blurs rushed across the cracked pavement, dodging the many sections cordoned off for rebuilding.

Hitomi and Jack arrived at the Radford building. A large crowd of onlookers was standing behind the tape the City Guard had set up. Several soldiers stood at the ready just outside the building, a tank parked in front of all of them.
 Hitomi and Jack slowed down and weaved through the crowd to the soldier yelling through a megaphone.
 "For the last time," the soldier said, "this is an extremely dangerous situation! Keep your distance! The next one who comes too close will be arrested on sight!"
 The soldier turned away. Hitomi walked up and tapped the soldier on the shoulder. The soldier whipped back around.
 "Goddammit!" he yelled. He stopped when saw her standing there.
 "Oh, it's you." he said. "Don't do that. Get over here. I'll take you to the lieutenant."
 The soldier led Hitomi and Jack past the others to the front near where the tank was parked. As she got closer, she could see there a

big hole blown in the side of the building. Three dead bodies were sprawled out in front of it. They were torn to shreds. Once upon the time, the sight of those mangled carcasses would have made Hitomi gag, but by now she'd seen things a thousand times worse.

"Lieutenant," the solider said to the man in uniform next to the tank. Lt. Rodriguez turned to them.

"Ah! Good, you're here. I guess Jack here filled you in on what happened," he said.

"Most of it. Any idea if anyone innocent is still alive in there?" Hitomi said.

"We're not sure, but we're pretty certain there is," Lt. Rodriguez said. "It's why we haven't just shelled the place until there's nothing left. Better to lose the building than let those lunatics and that freak get away. But we can't risk it if anyone else is still alive. That's why we're sending you in."

"Careful lieutenant," she said. "I'm one of those 'freaks' too."

"You're not anywhere near this, baby," he said. "This Neohuman's a Stage Five. I have no idea how those G.E.T guys got this thing here without it tearing them apart. It's been running loose in there and killing everyone in sight. We've got snipers taking shots through the windows, but they don't even faze it."

Stage Five was the worst of the Neohumans. They were more beast than human in appearance and behavior and were incredibly hostile, driven by base hunger and nothing else. Hitomi herself was a rare Stage Three. Her mutation during the Great Collapse had changed her profoundly but she had full control of it and maintained all her senses. Like most of the known Stage Threes, she'd been recruited by the New Federation of City-States as a soldier. Hitomi preferred to think of herself as a superhero rather than a soldier though. It offered little solace, but in times like this, you take what you can get.

She nodded to the lieutenant. "If there's anyone alive, I'll get them out."

With that, she transformed. It brought to mind a werewolf movie the way her nails and teeth sprang out like switchblades. A wispy layer of hair appeared on her arms, hair, and cheeks, and her limbs extended. By the time she had finished, she towered over Lt. Rodriguez, who was normally a head taller than her. The red leotard she wore had gained two more rips, clinging tightly on to her now much larger body.

With Jack by her side, she stomped into the Radford building.

As Hitomi entered the lobby, the smell of blood hit her hard. Mutilated bodies, torn up limbs, and intestines were littered about. Much of the furniture had been destroyed and the cubicles nearby had been flattened. Bullet holes were in the walls and floor. Hitomi shook her head and headed towards the counter. She saw that a hole had been torn in the ceiling behind it. Before she had a chance to investigate it, she heard gunshots. She ran toward the sound and found it was coming from the vault. The door was open and she saw a man in fatigues and a balaclava with his back turned to her standing in the doorway. She saw he was holding an AK-47. She approached him slowly.

    Just before she got to him, a similarly dressed man further in the vault shouted to him and pointed to her. He quickly turned around to face her. It was too late. She grabbed his head and slammed it hard against the wall. He slid into a heap on the floor, his blood leaving a streak on the vault wall. She turned to the other man in the vault. He was standing next to a group of tellers and customers kneeling on the ground. They were all clearly frightened. One woman lay on the ground with a fresh gunshot wound in her forehead. A young boy was crying over her body.

He started firing on Hitomi. The bullets hitting her felt like people flicking her with their fingers all over her body. She advanced towards him quickly. Seeing that his gun wasn't working on the Neohuman woman in front of him, he turned it towards the crowd.

"Stop, heathen! Leave now or I'll shoot them all!" he said.

Hitomi stopped and raised her hands. She started to back away. While the G.E.T cultist was focused on her, Jack sprinted between her legs. He leaped at the cultist's throat and bit it out. The cultist squeezed the trigger, but the burst of gun fire hit the wall.

Jack spat out the man's flesh and blood. "Piece of shit. He must have been trying to win some conversions and shooting those that refused," Jack turned to Hitomi. "I'll watch these folks. You go take care of the rest of these crazy fucks and the Neohuman."

"Right. I'll be back soon," she said.

As Hitomi exited the vault, Jack started licking the face of the boy crying over the dead woman, trying to comfort him.

Hitomi had climbed up six floors. Each one of floors reeked of blood. It was times like this she hated her enhanced sense of smell. She encountered G.E.T members on each of the floors. They impotently fired on her and she sent them all to the heaven they were working for. She slashed at them, caved in their skulls, tore them half. With every floor she got more vicious to the cultists as she got angrier from the carnage she witnessed on each one. She kept following holes in the ceiling, tracking the Stage Fiver.

The sixth floor was strangely clean and quiet. It had clearly been empty, even before the cult had shown up. Despite that, it smelled even worse than all the other floors. The blood was still there, but there was something else that she didn't recognize. She followed her nose to a corner office. A pool of blood was seeping out from under the door.

Hitomi threw the office door open. The stench was like a punch in the face. The room looked worse than the rest of the building. It was like someone had taken a paint roller and worked the place over with a bucket of blood. There were even more bodies here, but Hitomi saw that most of them were G.E.T members. Most were missing limbs or their head. Their intestines spilled out of their abdomens. A few looked like they had been split clean down the middle from the groin up. In the corner, the Stage Fiver sat gnawing on one of the bodies. It resembled a bird from the waist up, covered in feathers, a head like an eagle, talons for hands, and wings on its back. The lower half resembled a naked man's. Its legs were muscular and it sported a massive hard-on. It had clearly turned on the cult when it ran out of others to feed on.

The Stage Fiver looked up at Hitomi and let out a screech that rattled the windows, the dead cultist's guts falling from its beak. She clapped her hands over her ears. The smell and the sound disoriented her. By the time she realized the Stage Fiver was flying at her, it was too late.

The Stage Fiver knocked her on her back and swiped at her face with one of its talons. She cried out as it dug three deep cuts in her face, its claw barely missing her eye. It swung with its other talon, but Hitomi was able to crane her neck away from it. It still scratched her but not nearly as deep. As it was about to bring its other talon back down, she reached up and grabbed it. The Stage Fiver squawked in confusion.

Hitomi sent a hook right into its face. It would have been sent straight across the room had she not had a grip on it. Instead, it flopped hard right next to her. Its beak had nearly cracked in half from Hitomi's blow. She stood up, let its talon go, and brought her foot down on to its chest. Its body shook, still squawking, and it buried its claws in her calf muscle. She grit her teeth and winced, but pressed her foot down harder. She bent down and stuck her own claws in the Stage Fiver's feathery neck. It screeched louder and louder until, with one good yank, she pulled its head clean off.

The head went dead and silent right away, but the body went spastic. It shook like it was having a seizure, flapping its wings, flailing its arms and legs as blood sprayed out of the stump of its neck. Before it finally went limp, it ejaculated all over its own feathers.

Once upon a time, a sight like that would have made Hitomi throw up. Instead, she lifted the Stage Fiver's head up, spit in it, and tossed it aside. She limped over to the window and examined her face in her reflection in the window. The cuts on the one side of her face were deep, but they'd heal without any problems. She bent down and licked the wounds on her leg. The same was true of the bleeding holes in her calf. She'd suffered worse without even being scarred.

As she headed back down to the vault, she transformed back to her normal self. She figured after what the people in the vault at been through, they'd probably prefer to be lead out to safety by someone who at least looked like a normal human.

My Church

I grew up in a family that went to church every Sunday. I think our church was a little bit different, though.

Instead of a church building, our congregation met in the basement of an abandoned theater. We sat in folding chairs and the pastor's pulpit was a cheap, beat up looking lectern. The basement was lit with work lights hung up on the ceiling.

The pastor was really old. He looked like he was about eighty. He would start the service by having us bow our heads and pray for about ten minutes. After that, he would read a few chapters from his Bible. The problem was he usually forgot to bring it. When he did, he would pick up this moldy phone directory from the seventies that was always laying on the basement floor. He would read names and phone numbers from it for about half an hour.

When he was finished with that, he would pass out these hardcover hymn books. I think they were the result of some weird printing mistake. The cover had an English title that just said *Hymns*, but the inside was written all in Russian.

We didn't sing any hymns though. The pastor would kill the lights and we had to hit each other with the books. I was the only kid in the congregation, so it was easy to stay low and avoid getting hit. When I did get hit, it would really hurt and I'd sit on the floor and cry until it was over.

One day, I asked my mom what hitting each other had to do with God. She told me to ask the pastor. When I asked the pastor, he got really angry. He beat on his lectern and yelled, "The suffering of Christ is greater than yours!"

I suppose he was right. Getting hit with a book probably hurts a lot less than being nailed to a cross.

WATER MUSIC

Drink several glasses of water.

Sit cross-legged alone in a quiet room.

Rock back and forth.

Listen to the sound of the water sloshing in your belly.

Unreflected Text

A beat-up pickup truck with a flat tire drove by, sparks flying from the rim scraping on the road. It drove by an apartment building. In a second-floor apartment, José climbed off Linda.

Hey, bring your ass up here, he said.

He got on his back and she straddled his chest. He wrapped his arms around her waist and pulled her ass to his face.

Oh! Be gentle! she said.

José stuck his tongue in her asshole. Linda moaned. She grabbed his cock and jerked him off. He stuck his tongue in deeper. He sucked on her asshole. She took his cock in her mouth. He licked her asshole. She felt his cock swell. He came in her mouth. She felt his heavy breathing on her ass. He kissed her ass cheeks. She swallowed his cum.

Linda got up and put her arms around José's neck. She kissed him. He tasted his cum on her lips.

Linda and José curve and bend toward the headboard's empty frame like a reflection on the back of a spoon. They become silver and then liquid silver and flow in the headboard's frame. The mirror reflects a bed with no sweat, no indents, and no wrinkles in the sheets.

An old man comes in the room and lays on the bed. He looks at the reflection in the headboard's mirror.

The doctor said I have cancer, the old man says.

What kind? the reflection said.

Stomach.

Treatable?

It's too late now. Maybe if I'd gone in sooner.

I'm sorry to hear that.

I guess this is the end.

Yeah. It's been good working with you.

Yeah. Thanks for everything.

The old man rolls over and looks at the ceiling and waits to die. In the mirror, the old man got out of the bed.

The old man went into the bathroom and became a twenty-something man. The twenty-something man looked in the mirror. He picked his nose and ate his snot. He brushed his teeth. He combed his hair. He left the bathroom and came back with a gun. He put the gun in his mouth. He pulled the trigger. In the mirror, the back of the reflection's head bursts and sprays blood and brain meat into the tub behind him.

The twenty-something man puts down the gun and looks at the corpse in the mirror. He leaves the bathroom. He walks out of the apartment. There is a black void. The twenty-something man walks into the void. We watch from the door as he walks into the void. He becomes smaller and smaller until he is a dot in the distance. The dot disappears into the void.

The Akihabara Strangler

In the year 4016, the Empire of Japan's dominance over Asia was all but assured. India's army had been steamrolled over and Pakistan was already in talks to join the Empire with no resistance. Kazakhstan was in Japan's sights. It would give them a clear passage to Moscow, allowing them to bypass invading Russia through Siberia, a strategic blunder early in its campaign.

For its growing prosperity abroad, not all was well at home. The island had been divided into a minority of wealthy business owners, politicians, and military officers with everyone else living in conditions that ranged from what could barely be considered lower middle-class to absolute squalor. Crime, however, was at an all-time low, even in the worst slum of Tokyo, Akihabara.

Because of this, the string of brutal murders shocked the district's residents. Several women between their late twenties to mid-thirties had been found strangled to death with cords. Two of them had been pregnant. All of them were married, attacked at home while their husbands were at work.

Men had become afraid to leave their wives home alone, but none could afford to take the time off work. They were borderline slaves to their companies. The women of the district were forbidden from owning weapons and the black market for them had been stamped out by the iron boot of the Empire. The police had a stony indifference to a place like Akihabra. Most law enforcement had written off that part of the city as a dwelling for half-savages.

With the residents' inability to defend themselves and the complete apathy of the authorities, the Akihabara Strangler's reign of terror was able to continue unabated.

Please File Under Adult Contemporary

In the mid-1970s, record stores and radio stations around the country started receiving copies of a 12-inch single. The front of the sleeve was an overexposed black and white photo of someone with long hair looking out a window from behind. The back of the sleeve was solid black with nothing but the song names. Side A was called "Your Broken Heart." Side B was a cover of "Blue Moon." There were no artist credits for Side A, though Side B credited Richard Rodgers and Lorenz Hart as the original writers. The only other information was a small note that came with the records that read, "Please file under adult contemporary."

At the time, most store owners and DJs would only listen to the first minute of a single before deciding to sell or play it. Side A seemed to be a soft rock instrumental ballad. Side B was a piano solo rendition of "Blue Moon." Because of the lack of artist information, many of the places that received the records discarded them or put them in storage. Most of the record stores that received it followed the instructions and filed the record with the other adult contemporary records.

The few that listened to the record all the way placed it with the novelty records.

While "Your Broken Heart" begins as a normal soft rock ballad, it gets more chaotic as it goes on. It's also longer than one would expect, clocking in at 8 minutes and 51 seconds. Around the 3-minute mark, the song suddenly shifts to an arrhythmic drum solo. The drums then drop out completely and are followed by a racket that sounds like all the other instruments randomly playing the same note over and over again. The song then returns to a soft rock ballad, albeit a far different sounding one than the first 3 minutes. The ballad is interspersed with bursts of what's been described as free jazz improvisation. This continues until the last minute and a half. The music drops suddenly and a drone and the sound of heavy breathing take up the remainder of the track. Some who've listened to this part at high volumes have said they heard very quiet talking in the background as well, but were unable to make out what was being said.

The cover of "Blue Moon" on the B-side is also unusual. It goes on for 6 minutes and 4 seconds, almost twice the length of other renditions. The song goes as usual until the about 2-minute mark. At this point a mistake in the playing is made. For almost 3 minutes, the sound of angry pounding on piano keys and pained screaming goes on. People who have listened to this track have described this part as "blood curdling" and "very disturbing." The pounding and wailing gives way to quiet weeping until suddenly cutting off at the end of the track.

Very few bought the record and even less listened to it more than once. Many who blindly bought it either angrily returned the record to the stores or threw it away. It did find a small niche audience, especially among fans of experimental music.

One music critic who specialized in reporting on fringe musicians described it as "a clever deconstruction of music made for mass appeal." A few months after writing the review, the critic began to refuse to eat. The reason he gave when pressed was, "Nothing tastes right anymore." Despite the efforts of his family and doctor, the critic died of malnourishment.

A late-night radio DJ whose show revolved around comedy and novelty songs occasionally played both sides of the record. He would say that the record was "a funny joke, despite being made entirely at the listener's expense." Over the next year, the DJ became increasingly lethargic and indifferent. He was eventually fired for going on the air and saying, "I don't give a shit about this fucking show anymore," and then sitting in silence for the remainder of the show's time. Shortly after, he disappeared and was never heard from again. It's also notable that during the time he began playing the record, the area his show aired in had a large spike in suicides and traffic accidents.

    The records themselves are now rare collector's items, going for hundreds of dollars on sites like eBay. MP3s of the songs are unusually hard to come by and difficult to find due to the generic names of the tracks and the lack of any artist information. It seems like people who come into possession of the songs don't usually have much motivation to upload them to the Internet.

    Or to do anything at all.

Sharp-Tongued

The carnival's most popular attraction is a young man with a razor for a tongue. He looks to be about 17 or 18 years old. He has a handsome face and short, light brown hair. Men and women stand in lines longer than the carnival grounds to make out with him. His razor tongue runs across the inside of their mouths and cuts their lips, tongues, the roofs of their mouths, and scrapes their teeth. These people walk away with blood dripping from their mouths and mad with lust. There is a tent nearby where participants can masturbate or have sex afterwards. They are not allowed to go beyond making out with the razor-tongued young man. They can put their arms around him but they may not touch his ass or genitals. There is a large, muscular bouncer nearby who enforces the rule. Many times, he has had to beat to death someone who has broken the rule. Their bodies are taken away to be ground up for meat for the carnival's corn dogs.

There Goes the Neighborhood

Back when I was a kid, I lived in a neighborhood where most people kept to themselves. I didn't really know anyone there and all my friends lived on the other side of town. Not my parents though. They were close to the neighbors in the house next door. They would come over to our house all the time. They didn't have any kids for me to play with, so I was usually pretty bored.

I would sit there watching TV while my parents would talk with them. I never really paid attention to them.

Except that one night.

I noticed that they had suddenly gone quiet, so I turned to them to see what was up. They were all staring at me. I began to feel nervous, and I wondered if I had done something wrong.

Suddenly, their eyes started rolling around in ridiculous ways. They were facing in opposite directions and not focusing on anything at all. They began to babble in complete nonsense. I didn't know what had happened to them. All I knew was I had to get out of there.

I ran across the street. There was an old guy who lived alone in the house there. I was sure he could help. I banged on his door and he answered in pajamas and a ratty robe.

"What's the matter?" he said.

"My parents and their friends. They're..." I started sobbing. "I don't know what's wrong. I think they want to kill me. I don't know. Please help."

He got a terrified look on his face. He started breathing heavily and looking around. I was confused.

"What's wrong?" I asked.

He started sobbing too.

"My victim," he said, "I buried him." He pointed at the ground. "Down there. He suffered."

I didn't wait for him to explain. I ran away. I decided to run down to the house at the very end of the street. I don't know why. For some reason, I thought whoever lived there could help me. I banged on the door and a guy who looked like he was in his early twenties answered.

"What do you want?" he asked me.

I was really panicking but I managed to explain what happened with my parents, their friends, and the old guy across the street.

"Shit!" the guy said. "All right, come in here."

I went in and closed the door behind me. The guy walked over to the hallway and shouted down it. Another guy who looked about the same age came into the living room. The first guy told him what I said to him.

"Fuck!" the second guy said. "It's happening sooner than we thought it would!"

"What? What's happening?" I said.

"Never mind," the second guy said. "Just wait here, we'll be back in just a sec."

The two guys went down the hall. I stood there in the living room for about ten minutes, but it seemed like forever. The two guys came back wearing backpacks and one of them was carrying a briefcase.

"All right, let's get going," the first guy said. "Open the door."

I felt safe with these two for some reason. They were like cool big brothers. I turned around, opened the door, and stepped outside. It took me a moment to process what I saw.

Everyone in the neighborhood was outside and in the street. They were all naked and having sex. Very violent sex. The first man and woman I spotted I saw that the woman had stuck her fingers in the man's eye and was rooting around in the bleeding hole. While she was doing that, the man was beating her face and smashing her head on the asphalt. Another man was tearing a woman's ears off while she bit off his lips. All around them, there were huge puddles of this white fluid that looked like semen.

I just froze and gaped at the scene in front of me. Then, in the blink of an eye, everyone and the white fluid disappeared without a trace. Dumbfounded, I turned around to the two guys. Right before my eyes they turned into naked women. Before I could react, they disappeared like the others. The things they were carrying were gone too.

It was all too much. I just curled up in a ball on the ground and cried. I don't know how long I was sitting there crying when the police cars pulled up. One of cops ran up to me and asked me if I was hurt. Somehow, I was able to raise my head enough to shake it.

The cops took me down to the station and asked me what happened. I ran down everything from my parents and their friends to everyone disappearing. One of the cops looked at another with a confused look on his face.

"There must be something seriously wrong with this boy," he said.

"Hey, I don't see a reason not to believe him," the other cop said. "We searched that whole damn street and didn't find a trace of anyone but this kid. That many people just up and disappearing? Something weird happened there."

They never found my parents or anyone else who disappeared. I got sent to a foster home. Somehow, I managed to have a mostly normal life afterwards. However, I haven't had a single good night's sleep since.

I still wonder what the hell happened. What made my parents act like that? Where did they all go? Did something take them? Why didn't it take me too? Did it leave me behind on purpose, or was it a mistake?

And if it was, will it come back for me?

RealDoll Ballet

The stage is dominated by a giant screen. It flickers on. Static illuminates the nude RealDolls littered in front of the screen. They slowly rise like marionettes being pulled by strings. The sound of white noise gradually increases as the RealDolls move about the stage in some grotesque parody of a ballet.

There is a loud bang as the door of the theatre is thrown open. Ken rushes past the empty rows of seats to the stage. He is screaming something but the sound of the white noise drowns it out. The RealDolls continue dancing, indifferent to his presence. He tackles the first one in his path. He grabs its head and bashes it into the floor repeatedly. The head eventually rips off its body. Ken puts his foot on the decapitated RealDoll's body and tears its leg out of the socket.

Ken begins to knock over and destroy every RealDoll on the stage. The Dolls continue to dance, unaware of the man among them. He beats them with the leg. He kicks their heads in. He stomps holes in their chests and guts. He tears their skin off, revealing their metal skeletal frames. As each Doll is destroyed, the white noise gradually becomes quieter. Ken's screams and grunts can finally be heard. When the last RealDoll is destroyed, the only thing that can be heard in the theatre is Ken's heavy breathing.

Ken tosses the leg aside and falls to his knees. He begins to sob. He looks stage right and crawls over to it among the remains of the RealDolls. He reaches offstage and pulls a USB cord towards himself. He reaches in his pocket and pulls out a smartphone. He continues to sob as he presses the screen several times. He plugs the USB cord into the phone.

The giant screen flickers. The static dissipates. In its place appears a photo of a young woman of around 20-years-old standing on a beach. She is looking over her shoulder and smiling at the camera. Ken looks up at the screen and his sobbing ceases. He crawls up to the screen and places his hand on it. He lets his head fall onto the screen and begins to loudly weep.

John Walks into a Bar

John leaves the private viewing booth he lives in. He has to walk four miles to leave the booth area and enter the magazine section. He walks past aisles dedicated to amputees in diapers, vintage kiddy porn, car crashes, and horses in Nazi uniforms. Each aisle is two miles long. The floor under John's shoes is crunchy with dried semen.

John turns down an aisle dedicated to Latina MILFs. He walks past the men who are looking at the magazines and jacking off. One man turns around as John approaches and cums on his pants. "Hehe. Sorry!" the man says.

John sighs. He grabs a magazine off the shelf and wipes the semen off his pants with it. He tosses the magazine on the floor. He walks until he comes to the middle of the aisle. There is a sign in the shape of a bar floating parallel to the ground. It is as high as John's forehead. John walks into the bar. Fake booze bottles rattle. "Ouch! Shit!" John says.

John rubs his forehead. A bruise forms. John pushes the bruise like a button. He winces in pain. A green door drops from the bar like a projector screen. John opens the door. It leads to a descending staircase. John walks down the staircase. He steps over a dog sleeping on one of the steps. The staircase ends at another green door. This door has a sign above it that says "Smegma Bill's Tavern."

John enters the tavern. There is a real bar inside. "Don't Be Cruel" by Elvis Presley is playing on the jukebox. John walks up to the rail where a man is watching a football game on the TV.

"Excuse me, are you Smegma Bill?" John says. The man turns to John.

"Yup. That'd be me. I don't open for another hour, but you're welcome to pull up a stool and watch the game."

"Actually, I'm here about that dishwasher position."

"Oh, yes. What's your name?"

"John."

"Okay. Come with me, John."

Smegma Bill leads John to the kitchen.

"No interview or anything?" John says.

"What for?" Smegma Bill says. "You don't need a bachelor's degree and a three-year internship to wash dishes."

"I guess not."

"You seem sane and smart enough. My daughter used to wash the dishes, but she's gone off to college. Don't do anything really stupid and we'll get along fine."

"Okay."

Smegma Bill shows John where the sink is, where the dish soap is and where all the dishes go.

"My wife does all the cooking," Smegma Bill says. "She'll be here soon. I'll introduce her."

A young man walks into the kitchen. He wears a cowboy hat and carries an acoustic guitar with no strings.

"Ah, you're here early. John, this is my son. His name is Billy Jr.," Smegma Bill says. "Billy, this is John. He's our new dishwasher."

"Um, hi," John says. He finds himself staring at Billy's stringless guitar.

Billy opens his mouth. Guitar music comes out.

"My son's a born musician," Smegma Bill says. "He's going to be performing later tonight. Go ahead and get started on the dishes in the sink. I'm going to help him carry in his sound equipment."

Billy sets down his stringless guitar. He and Smegma Bill leave the kitchen.

John goes over to the sink and puts dish soap in it. He turns on the water. As the sink is filling, he looks over at the stringless guitar. He starts breathing heavily. He feels his hard-on growing. He looks at the kitchen door then walks over to the guitar. He starts to caress the guitar. He kisses the neck. He feels the wooden body of the guitar. He rubs his face over it. He feels the area around the sound hole. He sticks his hand in the hole.

John feels his body shrinking. He presses himself against the stringless guitar. He licks and kisses its wooden body.

When he is small enough, he climbs inside the sound hole.

He curls up at the bottom of the inside of the guitar.

He feels as if he is cuddling with a lover.

He feels safe.

He forgets that he lives in a private viewing booth in an adult bookstore the size of a city.

He forgets walking on semen-encrusted floors.

He forgets that washing dishes is the only job he could find.

He forgets that anything bad could ever happen to him.

He forgets that anything could ever happen to him.

He forgets that he has a body.

He is shaken out of this state by a loud knocking noise. He is thrown around as someone shakes the guitar. He falls out through the sound hole. He returns to normal size when his body hits the floor.

He stands up and sees Smegma Bill and Billy.

Billy is holding the guitar. He opens his mouth. Discordant guitar music comes out.

"Just what in the hell were you doing?" Smegma Bill says.

"I was just. I," John says.

"Not only are you a goddamn pervert, you let the goddamn sink overflow!" Smegma Bill points at the sink. There is a puddle of soapy water on the floor around it. "You weren't even here an hour and you already fucked up. Get the hell out of here. You're fired. Don't ever come back."

John leaves the kitchen and then the tavern. He walks up the staircase. He forgets about the dog and steps on it. It wakes up and bites his ankle. He kicks the dog. It runs down the stairs. He gets to the top of the staircase. He goes through the door. The green door raises back up into the floating bar.

He walks up the aisle. He looks at the magazines. One of the magazines has a woman whose body reminds him of the shape of the guitar. He grabs the magazine. He unzips his pants and takes out his hard-on. He jacks off until he cums on the magazine. He tosses the magazine on the floor. He walks back to the private viewing booth where he lives.

Cathy

Everybody calls him Cathy. He's not easy to miss. He's a brutally ugly crossdressing man who's always wearing bright red dresses, sweaters, hot pants, hats and so on. He's bald and usually goes out as such, but occasionally he'll wear an unnaturally red wig. Even if you don't notice him, he'll make you.

    He has this stunt he keeps pulling for attention. You'll often see him writhing around on the ground with fake blood and a mannequin limb next to him, acting like he's just lost an arm or a leg. It looks like he's actually injured from a distance, but you can tell it's fake when you get up close. That's usually when pops he up and laughs at you. There have been several times someone's called 911 on him and he ended up arrested. He was always back doing his shtick in a few weeks though.

    One day, a friend and I came across him sprawled on the ground in a puddle of his stage blood and a fake arm next to him. He screamed at us to help him and that his arm had been cut off. We weren't in the mood to deal with his shit and just kept walking past. He started screaming that we were horrible, heartless people. He jumped up and chased after us. We started running. We had no idea what a nut like him would do if he got violent.

The whole time he chased us, he just kept yelling that we were awful people who didn't care if he died. He reached into the bright red purse he was carrying and pulled out a gun. That got us running even faster. He pointed the gun at himself though. When he pulled the trigger, we heard the click. The gun was empty. He just kept pulling the trigger. Click click click. The whole time he was yelling and shaking his head like he was angry he couldn't blow his brains out.

As soon as my friend and I were safely in my house with all the doors locked, we called the police. When they arrived, they found him waving the gun around and banging on my front door. They cuffed him, put him in the car, and questioned us about him.

They took him away and I haven't seen him around since. They must have put him away in a prison or nut house for good this time.

Little Jimmy's Secret

Little Jimmy's parents sat in the living room reading. Jimmy came into the living room, went up to his father, and tugged on his sleeve. "Dad?" he said.

"What is it Jimmy?" Jimmy's father said as he turned his head. "You're supposed to be in... HOLY SHIT!" he said and froze when he saw Jimmy.

"What's the matter hon... OH MY GOD!" Jimmy's mother said as she looked up.

Jimmy's skin was rotting all over. Green and black discoloration covered his entire body and large chunks of it seemed to be peeling off. Jimmy's dad stood up. He held out his hands but was afraid to touch his son.

"Dad," Jimmy said. "I had a secret."

Jimmy reached up and tore the skin off his head in strips. Underneath, Jimmy's head was still there. It looked like his head was back to normal, other than the fact it was transparent.

"I died while I was inside Mom," Jimmy said. "I didn't want to make you sad, so I put my skin over my ghost."

Jimmy's mother gasped and held her hands over her mouth.

"It's going bad. The skin went bad," Jimmy said. His head became more transparent. "My ghost is going away. I'm sorry I didn't tell you."

Jimmy's father moved closer to his son as he started fading. "Jimmy..."

"I'm sorry. I love you both," Jimmy said.

As Jimmy's father went to hug his son, he disappeared, leaving nothing but an armful of decaying flesh. Jimmy's father threw the skin to the ground in disgust and despair.

He looked at his wife. She was clutching her stomach. She stood up and walked towards the bathroom. He saw there was blood running down the inside of her legs.

"What's wrong, dear?" he said.

"I feel like I'm having contractions," she said.

"What!? Should I call 911?"

"Help me into the bathroom first."

He took her by the arm and rushed her into the bathroom. She took her bloodstained underwear off and pulled up her dress. She sat in the tub with her legs spread.

"Something's coming out. Hold my hand," she said.

He did so.

She felt a sharp pain.

A rancid soup of blood, pus, muscle tissue, and bone splinters poured out of her vagina. A rotten smell filled the bathroom.

She screamed.

Her husband retched, turned away, and covered his mouth and nose.

The soup flowed across the tub and into the drain.

Why You Should Always Tip the Pizza Guy

Good evening! I'm calling to inform you that your pizza may arrive later than expected. Our deepest apologies, but your delivery driver has fallen into a wormhole. Currently, he is navigating a maze of holes in reality to bring you your pizza as soon as possible. We have also been informed that a man wearing a mask that resembles a Kandinsky painting has been placing various obstacles in his path. Rest assured, our drivers have been trained to navigate such things with ease. We appreciate your business and we hope you will enjoy your pizza when it arrives. Thank you!

Last Night I Dreamt of Hell and High Waters

There's a reason I'm living in this abandoned warehouse. It's not because I'm a drunk or drug addict. It's not because I'm mentally ill either. Though people might think I am.

You see, it began about a month ago with a dream I had. Well, I don't even know if it was a dream. I don't know what else to call it.

In this dream, I found myself on a fishing boat. The boat was decrepit and rusty. There was a giant crane in the middle of the deck holding a net. The crew looked like normal fishermen for the most part. Except there was something awful about their eyes. Have you ever looked someone in the eyes after you made them extremely angry? These fishermen looked like that all the time.

The surrounding ocean was an unnatural green and looked more like sludge than ocean water. The sky was covered in clouds that were the same green as the ocean with areas of rust red in the cracks of the clouds.

They dropped the crane into the water and left it in there for a short time. Then they pulled it up and let the net drop their catch all over the deck.

But there were no fish. There was only garbage.

And bodies

Bodies of infants

Many of them looked torn apart. A few were still alive, twitching and making gurgling sounds. The deck was soaked with their blood and viscera.

I was so frightened and disgusted that I accidentally backed right off the deck and fell overboard.

The sludge water felt indescribably gross. I started thrashing and panicking. The fishermen dropped the crane back in the water. I swam over to it and grabbed on to the rope.

That's when I woke up.

I was disturbed, yes. But I shrugged it off pretty quickly. After all, it was just a dream.

Famous last words.

I went about my day. However, not long after, I started hearing laughter. It would start very quiet and distant sounding. Then it would get gradually louder until it was like someone howling right in my ears. Then it would suddenly stop.

I tried waiting for it to go away. It wouldn't. After two weeks, I was still hearing it several times a day and I couldn't sleep because it kept waking me up.

I knew it wasn't real. Nobody else around me heard it. But I had to prove it to myself. I got a tape recorder and waited for the laughter to start up. Then I pressed record. After the laughter stopped I rewound the recorder and pressed play.

I heard it!

The laughter was coming from the recorder!

The laughter was fucking real!

I knew I had to run. I had to get away from whatever it was.

I dropped everything and went to my mother's house. I told her I couldn't explain, but I needed to stay with her for a while. She probably thought I committed a crime and was hiding out. Either way, she let me stay. Bless that woman.

For about a month, I didn't hear anything. I thought I lost whatever it was.

But then it started again. The laughter.

Without telling my mother, I left her house and skipped town.

That's why I'm here now.

It's been three weeks and it hasn't found me yet. I know it will soon and then I'll have to run again.

That's how it is. If you think I'm crazy or you don't believe me, I have nothing left to say to you.

Deep Sea Diving Suit

Jeff has difficulty holding down jobs. There are few places with a dress code that allows deep sea diving suits. There have been very few occasions where he got past the interview stage. Most HR people are put off when a guy walks in wearing a diving suit. Even the occasions where he does get a job, the heaviness and awkwardness of the suits always get in the way of his duties. As such, he is often dismissed from those places very quickly.

Jeff's social life is not very good either. The helmets on his suits make conversation hard. Many find it awkward interacting with Jeff because they can't see his face through the helmets, they muffle his voice, and the giant gloves make shaking hands uncomfortable. Guys don't like to hang out with Jeff because they find his clumsy and ridiculous movements from just trying to walk around in the suits embarrassing to be around.

Needless to say, Jeff's love life is practically non-existent. A deep sea diving suit does not flatter a man at all. Women tend to be very put off when they're approached by him. His only relationship petered out very quickly. His ex cited his reluctance to take off his diving helmet during sex as the deal breaker.

Often, Jeff has contemplated selling his diving suits in order to buy more normal clothes. While he is aware that this would make his life easier, there is some psychological block that keeps him from taking this simple action. It seems like he is unable to comprehend on a deep level that there could be a place that does not require constant protection from one's surroundings. He is so used to spending time in an environment hostile to his survival, that he finds himself unable to leave his protective suits despite the fact they make existing in a welcoming environment difficult.

Human Roach

I come home from work and he is going through my kitchen cupboards. He is eating my cookies.

I turn on the light and he ducks under the table like an earthquake drill. I grab the roach spray from the under the sink.

I drag him out from under the table by his antennae. I spray him in the face and he coughs and spits. I spray until his eyes roll back in his head.

I drag him outside. His wings tear off and his blood smears on the pavement. I throw his body head first into a garbage can.

Alex Watches Television

Alex walks into his apartment. He sits on his bed. He looks at his television. He gets up. He presses the power button. The television comes on. Alex sits down.

There is a title card in Russian on the television. Alex cannot read it. It fades out. A black and white image of a soldier with a Soviet uniform comes on. The soldier reaches out. The camera pans back to reveal he is taking a baby from a woman. The woman cries. She tries to hold on to the baby. The soldier pulls it out of the woman's hands. The soldier holds the baby upside down by its leg. The baby loudly cries. The soldier takes out a pistol. He shoots the baby through the head. The baby goes silent. The woman screams. The soldier throws the baby on the ground. The woman cries and screams. The soldier shoots the woman through the head. The woman falls over on the baby's body. The soldier walks away. The camera stays on the bodies of the woman and the baby.

Alex gets up. He changes the channel. He sits down. The picture shows a young boy crying in a white void. He looks up at the camera. He crawls toward the camera. He puts his face against what seems like a pane of glass. It is like the boy is pressing against the screen from the other side. The boy sobs. He pounds his fist on the glass.

Alex gets up. He changes the channel. The picture shows surveillance footage. The footage shows a woman in a white gown dancing in an empty room. A composition by JS Bach is playing. Alex sits down. He watches the woman dance. The music changes to a composition by Pyotr Tchaikovsky. The woman continues to dance. The music stops. The woman sits down on the floor. The music starts again. It is a composition by Ludwig van Beethoven. The woman gets up. She continues to dance.

Alex gets up. He changes the channel. The picture shows static. Alex changes the channel. The picture shows static. Alex changes the channel. The picture shows a man sitting in a chair reading a newspaper in a boiler room. The newspaper is in Chinese. The man looks up from his newspaper. He gets up. He walks towards the camera. He reaches behind the camera. The picture becomes static.

Alex changes the channel. The picture shows the film *Taxi Driver*. The film is dubbed in a language Alex does not recognize. Alex changes the channel. The picture shows the dead woman and baby again. Both have decomposed. Alex stares at the screen. He reaches behind the television. He pulls up the power cord. It is not plugged in. Alex stares at the cord. He looks back at the screen.

I think I need a new TV, Alex thinks. He throws down the power cord. He turns off the television.

A Very Young Something with Wings

Three weeks ago, something fell from the sky and smashed into my car. Shattered the windshield and put a huge dent in the hood. Needless to say, it was dead when I found it. It looked like a guy with wings, so I assumed it was an angel. Figured it ran into something that knocked it out of the sky. Maybe caught a stroke or a heart attack in midair and was dead before it hit the ground. The same thing happened last year with an old angel crashing through someone's skylight and into their living room. This one looked pretty young though. Like 20 at the oldest.

    The police couldn't find any ID or anything on it. They called in a steward from the local angel's union, but he didn't recognize the body. He couldn't find anyone who looked like it in their records either. When the coroner got a hold of it and took off its clothes, he found there was nothing on its crotch. Just blank flesh like a Barbie or Ken doll. It looked male, but when they cut it open, they found a uterus. But when they cut the uterus open, they found a penis and testicles nestled in there like a fetus. So, at this point, they don't know if it's male or female or a hermaphrodite. They're not even sure if it's an angel, because there's never been one with insides like that.

They're doing all they can to spread news and pictures of the thing all over the Internet, TV, and the local newspaper. They're hoping someone who knew it when it was alive will come forward and they'll get some answers.

As for me, I guess I'm just stuck taking the bus until I get the money to fix the car.

War Criminal: A One Act Play for One Performer

A wash basin beneath a shattered mirror. Enter THE SOLDIER. He splashes water on his face.

THE SOLDIER: As long as I can remember, I've always feared losing my reflection. At a young age, I got the idea that the reflection was essential to something inside me. I don't know where that came from. All I knew was that losing it would be worse than death. Often in school, I would ask to use the bathroom when I didn't need to go. I would go in just to make sure my reflection was still there. When I signed up for the service after the war started, I always carried a pocket mirror. I told my colleagues that it was a good luck charm. I gave them some story about how my girlfriend gave it to me. Of course, that was a lie. Before and after every battle, I immediately had to check my reflection. To make sure it was still there. It always kept me calm. Even as the battles grew more brutal. Even as the winter came while we were behind enemy lines. During one battle, we were forced to retreat. I ended up separated from my platoon. I lost many of my supplies. Including my mirror. I wandered alone for two days. Nearly frozen and begging for death in my own mind. I could have already been dead as far as I knew. I couldn't check my reflection. My body felt like it was moving by itself. Finally, I came to a house deep in the woods. There was a man chopping wood out front. I knew he had to be one of the enemy. That's how I rationalize it. I took aim with my gun and splashed his brains into the snow. His wife and daughter must have heard the shot. They looked out and screamed. They ran to his body. I moved in closer and picked off the mother. Before the girl had a chance to run, I trained my gun on her. I moved toward her. She was frozen in fear. This young girl of about 14. That look of fear in her lovely young face. It stirred something inside me. I grabbed her by her hair and dragged her into the cabin. I did such horrible things to her over the next countless hours. I raped her multiple times. I violated her with my rifle. I pissed on her. I stubbed out cigarettes on her body. I sodomized her until her rectum bled. I kicked her stomach until she vomited. I broke her arms and her legs. Then, when night had fallen, I dragged her naked outside to her parents' bodies. I threw hot water on her. I taunted it would be the only thing to keep her warm through the night. Then I left her there as I went to sleep in one of the beds in the house. It all made sense. They were the enemy. The enemy deserved it. In the morning, I went outside. The girl had frozen to death, hugging her mother and father's corpses. A permanent grimace and that look of fear still in her eyes. I felt strangely satisfied. They were the enemy. The enemy deserved it. That girl didn't deserve it. How could I force myself to believe that? But the enemy deserved it. She was the enemy. She represented the enemy. Her whole family did. I went into their bathroom to look in the mirror. But as I saw the mirror, I realized I couldn't bring myself to look. I never wanted to look again. I realized I hated my reflection at that moment. I grabbed my rifle and shot the mirror. I'm still in that house in the middle of the woods. I don't know how long it's been. Days. Weeks. More than a month maybe? I haven't been out. I might need to hunt for something to eat. I don't want to go outside though. I'm waiting for someone to find me. My own men. The enemy. It probably doesn't matter. When they find those bodies. When they find out what I've done. I'll be convicted of war crimes. Atrocities. I won't try to defend myself. I can see it now. I'll be hung in front of a jeering crowd. In the nearest mirror, my reflection will stand independent of me. It will shake its head and walk away.

Exit THE SOLDIER. Snowstorm. Everything is buried.

<u>Love: A Parable</u>

Every morning, you wake up and you must go into That Room. Inside That Room there is a large and running Meat Grinder. On the other side of it, a Worm-like Monster lays on the ground with its mouth open. The Worm-like Monster makes horrible squealing noises.

You must stick your hand in the Meat Grinder. The pain is unbearable. The sound of your flesh tearing and your bones crunching is drowned out by the sound of the Meat Grinder and the Worm-like Monster's horrible squealing and your own screams. When your whole hand is gone, the Worm-like Monster is sated and stops its horrible squealing and you may go about your day. Your stump bleeds profusely but your hand grows back over time so that you can do this again the next day.

You do not want to do this routine, but you must. If you do not, the Men in Green Balaclavas come for you. They hold you down and saw your hand off by force. It is much worse when they take your hand, because they also beat you so badly you cannot walk the rest of the day. You have tried hiding from the Men in Green Balaclavas, but they always find you. The longer you manage to avoid them, the worse they beat you when they catch you.

You have tried to find a way to lessen the pain. You have tried tying a tourniquet around your wrist, but it did not help. You have tried drugs, but you have not found one that is strong enough to numb the pain without making you pass out before you stick your hand in the Meat Grinder. You have tried listening to soothing music as you stick your hand in, but it did not help.

You resign yourself.

One day, you meet someone with a bleeding stump similar to yours. You go up and ask them about it. They tell you how every morning they must get up and go into That Room. They tell you how they must stick their hand into the Meat Grinder. They tell you about the Worm-like Monster and its horrible squealing. They tell you about the Men in Green Balaclavas. You tell them you know of these things and how you must also endure them.

You complain to each other of having to endure this routine, but soon your conversation turns to more pleasant topics. You talk for so long that you both notice your hands have grown back. You hold hands with them and go back to your house together.

You wake up the next morning with that person next to you in your bed. You decide to go into That Room together. You hold hands and walk as quickly as you can to That Room before the Men in Green Balaclavas come.

You walk into That Room with your companion. The horrible squealing of the Worm-like Monster and the sound of the running Meat Grinder are so familiar to you both. You walk up to the Meat Grinder together. You both take a deep breath and plunge your clasped hands in.

For once it hurts just a little less for the both of you.

THE END

ACKNOWLEDGEMENTS

"The Country Musician" was published in *Spoilage,* Vol. 1

"The Arranged Marriage" was published on *Soft Cartel*

"... but i was reminded of ...," "A Very Young Something with Wings," "Channel 104 at 2:45 AM," and "My Church" were published on *Philosophical Idiot*

"The Soda," "Please File Under Adult Contemporary," and "Two Sentence Horror Story" were published on *CLASH Media*

"The Complete Idiot's Guide to Saying Goodbye" was published on *The Mustache Factor*

"Meth Lab Nursery" was published on *Keep This Bag Away from Children*

"Violent Bitch Hitomi" was published on *The 2015 New Bizarro Author Homepage*

"Sharp-Tongued," "Why You Should Always Tip the Pizza Guy," and "Human Roach" were published on *Bizarro Central*

"There Goes the Neighborhood," "Last Night I Dreamt of Hell and High Waters," and "Alex Watches Television" were self-published on the author's blog

"Little Jimmy's Secret" was published in *Ugly Babies (Volume 1)*

"Deep Sea Diving Suit" was published in *Pretty Owl Poetry,* Summer 2014

"War Criminal: A One Act Play for One Performer" was published in *Strange Behaviors: An Anthology of Absolute Luridity*

My deepest gratitude to the editors who previously published my work.

AUTHOR OF THE GUIDE

Ben Arzate lives in Des Moines, IA. This is his first short story collection. Find him online at dripdropdripdropdripdrop.blogspot.com

EXCHANGE WORDS WITH US:
NihilismRevised@outlook.com
www.facebook.com/NihilismRevised

NR-0016
ISBN: 9781723784996
First Printing by Nihilism Revised 2018
Copyright © Ben Arzate 2018
All Rights Reserved.